# Chinese patterns to colour

Illustration by David Thelwell
Designed by Emily Beevers
Written by Struan Reid

With thanks to Dr. Tian Yuan Tan,
University of London

# Chinese colours and patterns

The ancient Chinese were brilliant inventors, artists and craftspeople. Many of the inventions and crafts that we take for granted today were first developed by the Chinese thousands of years ago.

## Special colours

The artists and craftspeople used dazzling, bold colours in many of the objects they made. According to ancient Chinese tradition, certain colours represented particular qualities. These are some of the most important colours:

Red stands for fire,
and symbolizes good luck.

Green stands for wood,
and symbolizes good health.

Silver/white stands for metal,
and symbolizes purity.

Gold/yellow stands for earth.

## Shape and pattern

The same patterns and shapes appear in many Chinese designs. You can see flame and cloud patterns, and flowers such as peonies, on everything from porcelain plates to silk robes.

Chinese kites are made of brightly coloured paper and silk.

Peony

Flame pattern

Clouds

# Calligraphy

Ancient Chinese artists developed a style of writing called calligraphy. They painted flowing characters on paper and canvas using ink and thick brushes.

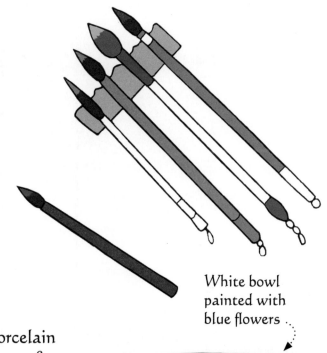

上海市

Chinese characters

White bowl painted with blue flowers

# Porcelain

The Chinese first started making porcelain about 2,000 years ago. They used a very fine clay to make delicate plates, vases and bowls. It was many centuries before people in other parts of the world learned how to do this.

# Silk and embroidery

Chinese weavers wove dazzling silk robes embroidered with rich patterns. Many of these were transported westward to Europe along a famous trade route known as the Silk Road.

This scene, from an early Chinese painting, shows women smoothing down a length of woven silk.

# Emperor and empress

For more than 2,000 years, until 1912, China was ruled by emperors. The emperor's wife was called the empress. Families of emperors are known as dynasties.

This empress's yellow hat is decorated with pearls and red and blue precious stones.

She is wearing flowing robes in yellow, blue, and red silk.

Blue silk ribbons

This is an emperor of the Qing dynasty (pronounced 'Ching'), that ruled China from 1644 until 1912. He is shown sitting on a golden throne.

Red and black hat with gold top

Yellow robes with blue, red and green patterns

Official seal, or stamp, of the emperor

# Fenghuang bird

This mythical bird was a symbol of happiness and harmony.

Long tail feathers in blue, green and red

Fenghuang birds were placed on the roofs of houses, to symbolize the happiness of the people inside.

Yellow beak, and red and blue head

Blue legs with yellow feet

# Houses and temples

Chinese houses and temples were often brightly painted and had roofs with dazzling green or yellow glazed tiles. Sometimes they had good luck figures on top.

# Music and song

At the Chinese emperor's court, small groups of musicians played on string or wind instruments.

Elaborate headdresses of red, green and gold

This musician is carrying a small type of harp.

Drum

This musician is playing a flute called a dizi (pronounced 'dee-tsu').

This musician is plucking the strings of a pipa (pronounced 'peepa').

# Peaceful landscapes

Landscape painting was one of the most important and popular kinds of Chinese painting. Artists often included little bridges, rocks and temples.

# Religions

Hundreds of gods and spirits played a part in the daily lives of the ancient Chinese people. One religion, Daoism, was first practised over 2,000 years ago.

Some of the gods and spirits were good, some bad. But all were treated with great respect.

The Jade Emperor, an important Daoist god, was ruler of Heaven and Earth.

He is holding a jade ball, symbolizing beauty and purity.

Red throne

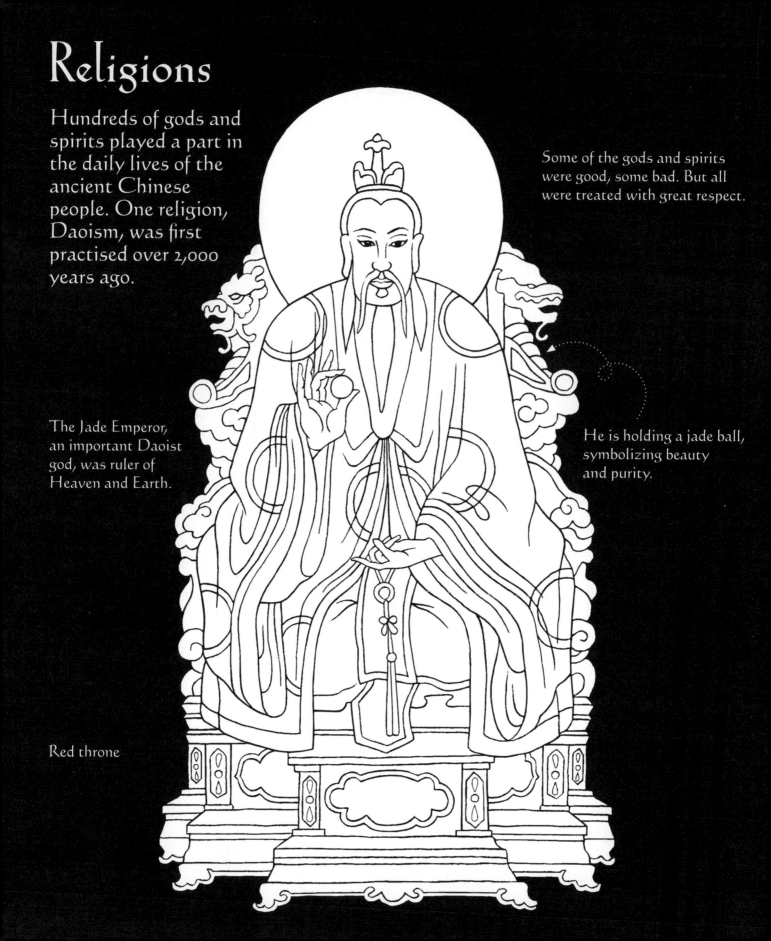

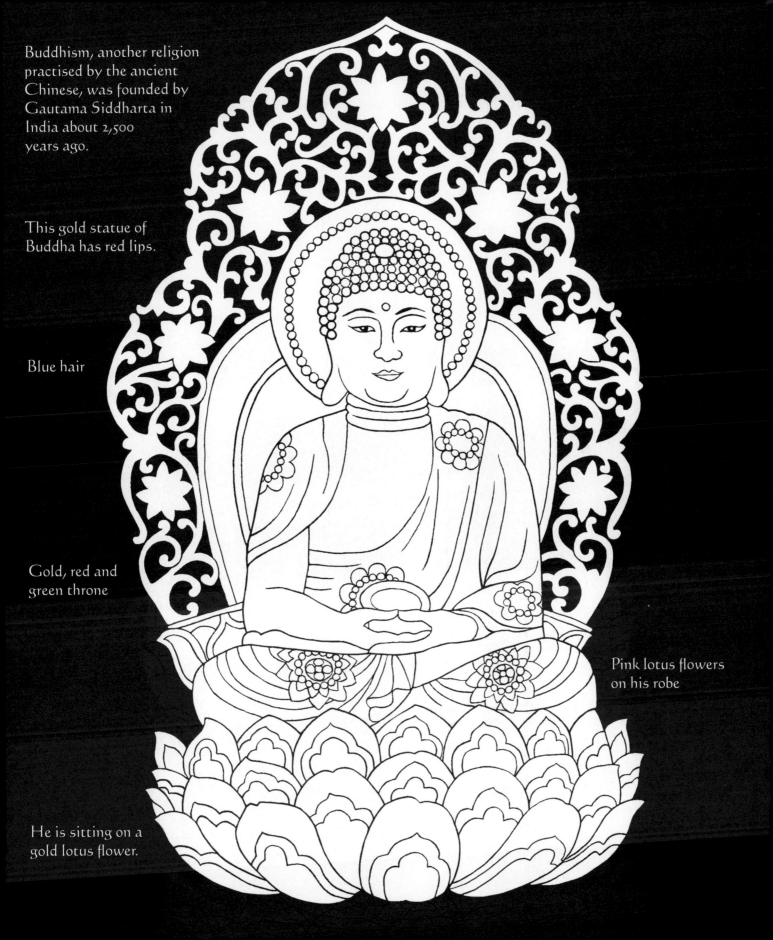

Buddhism, another religion practised by the ancient Chinese, was founded by Gautama Siddharta in India about 2,500 years ago.

This gold statue of Buddha has red lips.

Blue hair

Gold, red and green throne

Pink lotus flowers on his robe

He is sitting on a gold lotus flower.

# Into battle

Soldiers protected the Chinese empire from attack.
Many of them went into battle on foot, while others rode on horses.

This foot soldier is
armed with a long spear
and carries a quiver for
arrows on his belt.

His clothes are made of
coloured leather and steel.

His boots are made
of leather and thick
coloured felt.

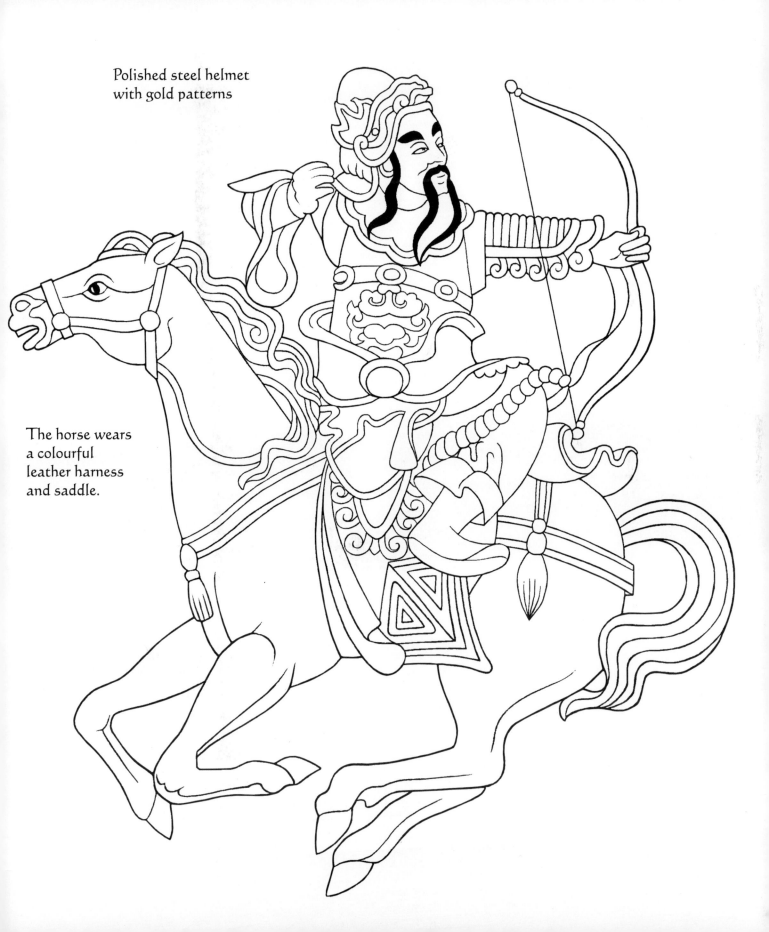

Polished steel helmet
with gold patterns

The horse wears
a colourful
leather harness
and saddle.

# Dragons

In ancient China, dragons were symbols of power, strength and good luck.

Each dragon has four legs, and feet with long, sharp talons.

The dragons chase flaming pearls of wisdom and truth.

Cloud patterns

Green and red scales

# Silk robes

The emperor and empress and their courtiers wore splendid silk robes embroidered with fancy patterns in all sorts of bright colours.

This purple robe was made for an empress. It is covered in flowers and butterflies, coloured red, green, gold and silver.

The empress wears a tall blue silk hat decorated in gold with red and blue precious stones.

Gold with white pearls

Red robe with cloud patterns...

...and dragon patterns.

# Porcelain

The word 'china' comes from the Chinese potters who first perfected the skill of making porcelain about 2,000 years ago. Different shapes and styles of decoration were used during different dynasties.

Green, red and yellow flower and leaf patterns

This enormous vase was made during the Qing dynasty.

The people are wearing yellow and blue clothes.

The walls of the vase are very thin, but they are also very hard and strong. It was designed to be placed on a table or on the floor.

Notice the cloud patterns.

Green base

This plate was also made
during the Qing dynasty.

Green, red and
yellow patterns

Brown birds on
a peony bush

Red and yellow flowers

# Chinese lions

Like dragons, lions stand for power and good luck. Carved stone male and female lions are still often placed outside buildings, to protect the people inside.

Notice
the flame
pattern.

This patterned ball represents unity and peace.
Male lions are often shown holding it under their paws.

# Writing with symbols

Chinese writing uses symbols, called characters, that represent both sounds and meanings. Words can be made up of one or more symbols.

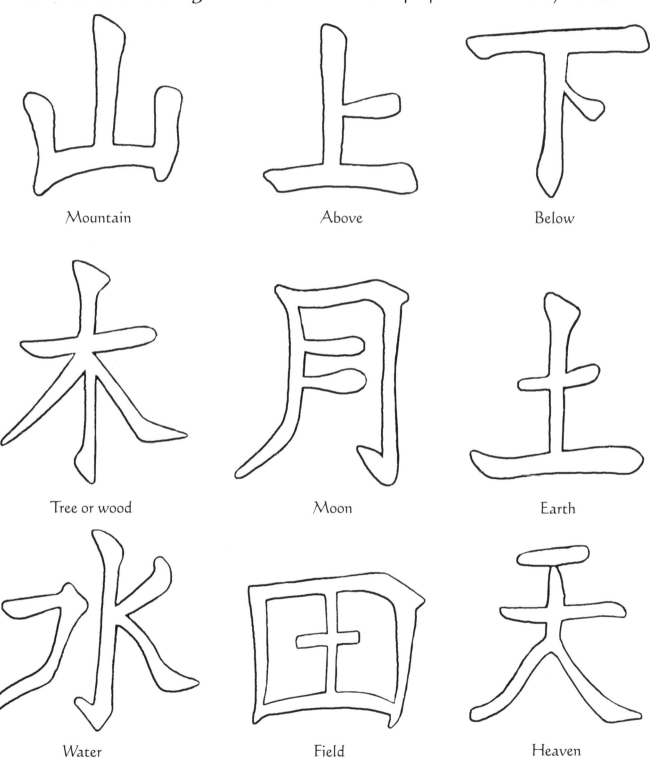

Mountain

Above

Below

Tree or wood

Moon

Earth

Water

Field

Heaven

# Chinese patterns

All the patterns on the next few pages are based on designs found on Chinese porcelain, embroidery and paintings and in the decoration of buildings. Look out for peony flowers and other popular patterns.

## Usborne Quicklinks

For links to websites where you can find out more about Chinese art, porcelain and embroidery, go to the Usborne Quicklinks website at www.usborne.com/quicklinks and enter the keywords 'Chinese patterns'. Please follow the internet safety guidelines at the Usborne Quicklinks website. We recommend that children are supervised while using the internet.